ULTIMATE STICKER COLLECTION

How to use this book

Read the captions in the 31-page booklet, then turn to the sticker
pages and choose the picture that best fits in the space available.
(Hint: check the sticker labels for clues!)

•

Don't forget that your stickers can be stuck down and peeled off again.

•

There are lots of fantastic extra stickers too!

LONDON, NEW YORK, MUNICH,
MELBOURNE, AND DELHI

Edited by Shari Last
Designed by Mark Richards
Jacket designed by Owen Bennett

First published in the United States in 2011 by
DK Publishing
375 Hudson Street,
New York, New York 10014

10 9 8 7 6 5 4 3 2 1
001–181146–Jun/11

Page design copyright © 2011 Dorling Kindersley Limited

LEGO, the LEGO logo, the Brick and Knob configurations,
and the Minifigure are trademarks of the LEGO Group.
©2011 The LEGO Group.
Produced by Dorling Kindersley Limited under license from the LEGO Group.

Color reproduction by Alta Image, UK
Printed and bound by L-Rex Printing Co., Ltd, China

Discover more at
www.dk.com
www.LEGO.com
www.warnerbros.com

Harry Potter

Harry Potter thinks he is just an ordinary boy, until he finds out that he is a wizard! In the wizarding world, Harry is known as "The Boy Who Lived."

Hedwig
Harry has a pet owl called Hedwig.

Uncle Vernon
Harry's uncle, Vernon Dursley, does not like magic.

Harry Potter
Harry has dark hair, glasses, and a lightning-shaped scar on his forehead.

Harry's Wand
Harry's wand has a phoenix feather core.

4 Privet Drive
Harry lives with his uncle, aunt, and cousin in a house at 4 Privet Drive.

Student Harry
Harry is in Gryffindor House at Hogwarts.

Hogwarts Express

Hogwarts students travel to school on board the Hogwarts Express. It departs from Platform 9¾ at King's Cross station.

9¾

Trunks
Hogwarts students pack their magical school supplies in trunks.

Ron Weasley
During their first year, Ron Weasley and Harry sit together on the Hogwarts Express.

Ready for School
Harry carries his owl Hedwig and all his school supplies on a trolley.

Food Trolley
Wizarding candy can be bought on board the Hogwarts Express.

Chocolate
Chocolate bars can be bought from the food trolley.

Luggage
Hogwarts students load their luggage onto the Hogwarts Express.

Hermione Granger
Harry meets Hermione Granger on board the Hogwarts Express.

Dumbledore's Chocolate Frog Card
Each pack of Chocolate Frogs contains a card about a famous witch or wizard.

Hogwarts Express 5972

Welcome to Hogwarts

Hogwarts School of Witchcraft and Wizardry is a castle with turrets and stained-glass windows. It has many secret passages, hidden rooms, and shifting staircases.

The Sorting Hat
The Sorting Hat sorts students into their houses.

Harry at Hogwarts
Harry Potter wears the Gryffindor crest on his uniform.

Four Houses
Hogwarts students are divided into four houses: Gryffindor, Slytherin, Ravenclaw, and Hufflepuff.

Ron at Hogwarts
Ron Weasley is in Gryffindor House, with Harry and Hermione.

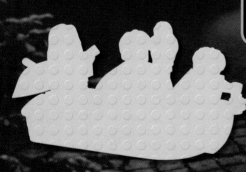

Boat to Hogwarts
New students travel by boat to Hogwarts castle.

Hogwarts Castle

Hogwarts Acceptance Letter

On Harry's 11th birthday, he receives a letter from Hogwarts School of Witchcraft and Wizardry.

Cauldron

Hogwarts students make their Potions in cauldrons.

Top of the Class

Hermione Granger is top in almost every class.

Draco Malfoy

Draco Malfoy is in Slytherin House.

Hogwarts Staff

Every class at Hogwarts has a different teacher. Students learn a variety of magic from their professors, from Potions to Transfiguration.

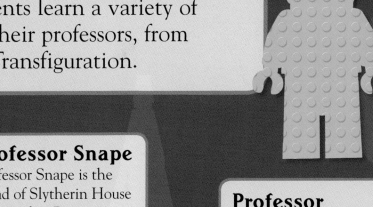

Professor Snape
Professor Snape is the Head of Slytherin House and teaches Potions.

Professor Dumbledore
Professor Dumbledore is the Headmaster during Harry's first six years at Hogwarts.

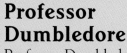

Professor Lockhart
During Harry's second year, Professor Lockhart teaches Defense Against the Dark Arts.

Professor Trelawney
Professor Trelawney teaches Divination at Hogwarts.

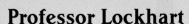

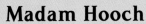

Madam Hooch
Madam Hooch is the Quidditch teacher at Hogwarts.

Professor Umbridge
During Harry's fifth year, Professor Umbridge teaches Defense Against the Dark Arts.

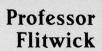

Professor Flitwick
Professor Flitwick teaches Charms class.

Professor Lupin
During Harry's third year, Professor Lupin teaches Defense Against the Dark Arts.

Professor McGonagall
Professor McGonagall is the Head of Gryffindor House.

Rubeus Hagrid
Hagrid is half-giant and the Keeper of Keys and Grounds at Hogwarts.

Hagrid's Hut

9

The Weasleys

The Weasley family lives at The Burrow. Mr. and Mrs. Weasley have six sons and one daughter.

Scabbers
Ron has a pet rat called Scabbers.

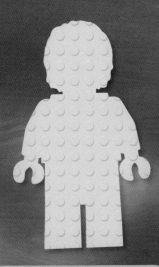

Molly Weasley
Mrs. Weasley is Ron's mother and a member of the Order of the Phoenix.

Ginger-Haired Ron Weasley
Ron has ginger hair —like the rest of the Weasley family.

Arthur Weasley
Mr. Weasley works for the Ministry of Magic and is interested in Muggle artifacts.

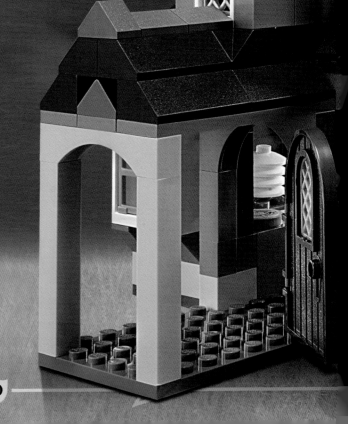

Weasleys' Flying Car
The Weasleys have a flying car.

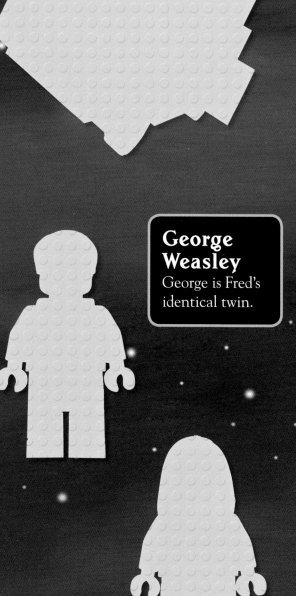

George Weasley
George is Fred's identical twin.

Fred Weasley
Fred is one of Ron's older brothers.

The Burrow

Ginny Weasley
Ron's younger sister is called Ginny.

Wizarding World

The wizarding world is filled with unique creatures, locations, and magical items. Harry and his friends are constantly amazed by the wonderful things that they encounter.

Gringotts

Goblin
Gringotts bank is run by Goblins.

GRINGOTTS BANK

Floo Network
Witches and wizards can travel to different locations using the Floo Network.

Wizard Treasure
Gringotts Goblins look after wizard treasure.

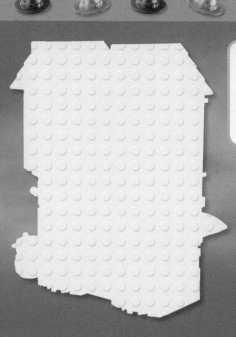

Diagon Alley
Diagon Alley is a street full of wizarding shops, including Ollivanders.

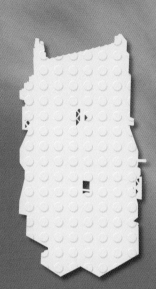

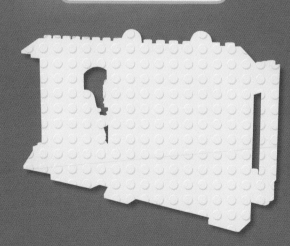

Mr. Ollivander
Harry buys his wand from wandmaker, Mr. Ollivander.

Wizard Pets
Wizards can buy pets in Diagon Alley.

The Shrieking Shack
The Shrieking Shack is in Hogsmeade.

Honeydukes
Honeydukes is a sweet shop in Hogsmeade.

Knight Bus
The Knight Bus is a purple, triple-decker bus that picks up wizards who are stranded.

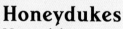

Stan Shunpike
Stan Shunpike is the conductor of the Knight Bus.

Charms and Spells

At Hogwarts, students learn to use charms and spells, such as *Wingardium Leviosa* and *Expelliarmus*. These spells are helpful to Harry and his friends during their adventures.

Sword of Gryffindor
The sword of Gryffindor first appears to Harry in the Chamber of Secrets.

Invisibility Cloak
Harry receives an Invisibility Cloak that used to belong to his father, James Potter.

Mirror of Erised
The Mirror of Erised shows Harry his greatest desire—to be with his family.

Transfiguration
Professor McGonagall teaches Transfiguration.

Remembrall
A Remembrall is a magical object that reminds you if you have forgotten something.

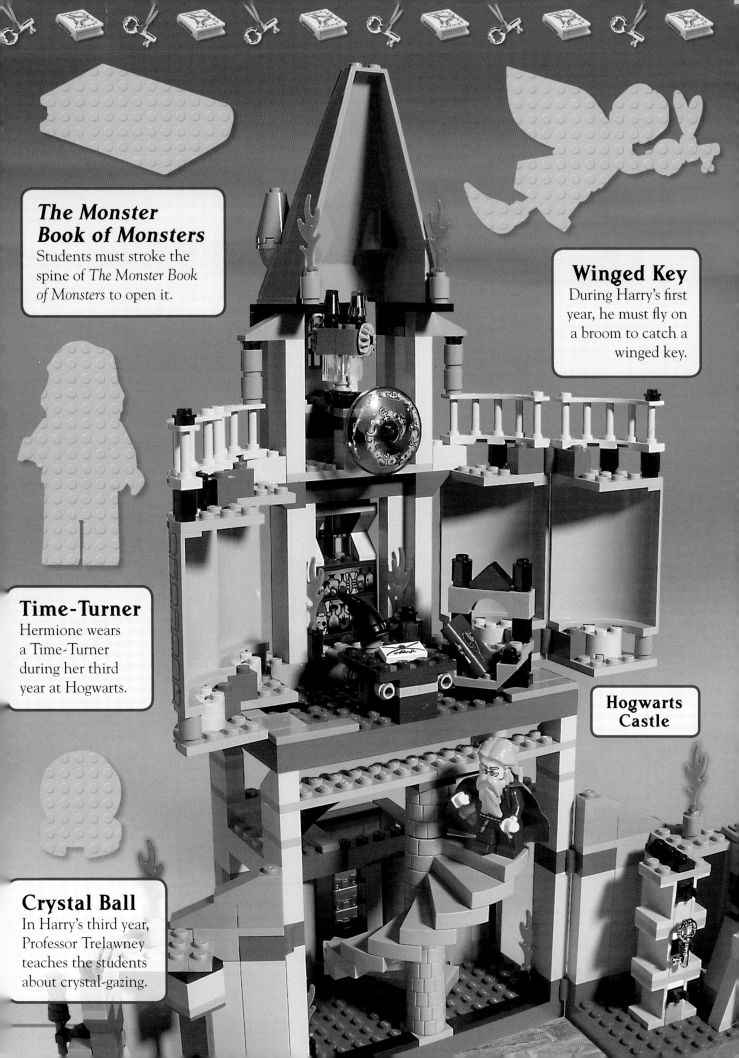

The Monster Book of Monsters
Students must stroke the spine of *The Monster Book of Monsters* to open it.

Winged Key
During Harry's first year, he must fly on a broom to catch a winged key.

Time-Turner
Hermione wears a Time-Turner during her third year at Hogwarts.

Hogwarts Castle

Crystal Ball
In Harry's third year, Professor Trelawney teaches the students about crystal-gazing.

Lord Voldemort

Lord Voldemort is known to be the most evil wizard of all time. He and his followers, the Death Eaters, terrorize the wizarding world.

Harry in Year Four
In his fourth year at Hogwarts, Harry battles Lord Voldemort in Little Hangleton graveyard.

Sorcerer's Stone
During Harry's first year at Hogwarts, Lord Voldemort tries to obtain the Sorcerer's Stone.

Lord Voldemort
Voldemort has white skin and a nose that is flat, like a snake's.

Tom Riddle's Diary
Harry destroys Tom Riddle's diary with a Basilisk fang.

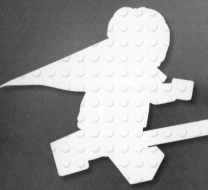

Professor Quirrell
During Harry's first year, Professor Quirrell teaches Defense Against the Dark Arts at Hogwarts, and he possesses a dark secret.

Tom Riddle
Harry meets Tom Riddle in the Chamber of Secrets.

Peter Pettigrew
Peter Pettigrew is a Death Eater who betrays Harry's parents.

Riddle's Tomb
Voldemort's father, Tom Riddle Senior, is buried in Little Hangleton graveyard.

Parseltongue
Lord Voldemort is a Parselmouth, which means he can talk to snakes.

A Graveyard in Little Hangleton

Life at Hogwarts

Hogwarts castle has many different rooms. Students must be careful as the staircases move!

Argus Filch
Mr. Filch is the caretaker at Hogwarts and has a pet cat called Mrs. Norris.

Suits of Armor
Suits of armor line the hallways of Hogwarts.

Neville Longbottom
Neville is in Gryffindor House with Harry.

Potions
Students at Hogwarts take Potions classes.

Marauder's Map
Harry is given a magical map that shows the location of everyone in Hogwarts.

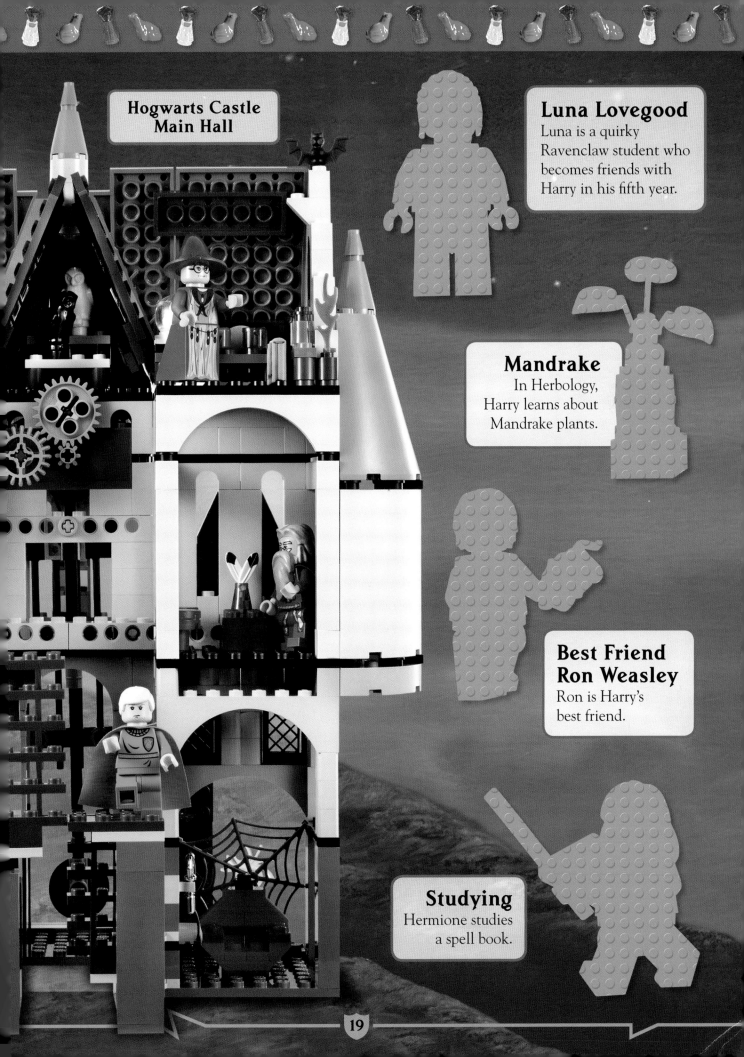

Hogwarts Castle Main Hall

Luna Lovegood
Luna is a quirky Ravenclaw student who becomes friends with Harry in his fifth year.

Mandrake
In Herbology, Harry learns about Mandrake plants.

Best Friend Ron Weasley
Ron is Harry's best friend.

Studying
Hermione studies a spell book.

Quidditch

Quidditch is the most popular wizard sport. Each house at Hogwarts has its own Quidditch team.

Seeker
Harry is the Seeker for the Gryffindor House Quidditch team.

Firebolt
In Harry's third year, he receives a Firebolt.

Quidditch Balls
There are four Quidditch balls: one red Quaffle, two black Bludgers, and one Golden Snitch.

Slytherin Seeker
Draco Malfoy is the Seeker for the Slytherin House Quidditch team.

Golden Snitch
The Golden Snitch is a small golden ball with silver wings that is very difficult to catch.

Oliver Wood
Oliver is the Captain of the Gryffindor House Quidditch team.

Quidditch Cup
Each house team at Hogwarts competes to win the Quidditch Cup.

Quidditch Helmet
Quidditch players wear a helmet as part of their uniform.

Marcus Flint
Marcus is the Captain of the Slytherin House Quidditch team.

Quidditch Tower

Goalposts
Keepers must defend their team's goalposts.

Quidditch Book
Quidditch Through the Ages is a book about the history of Quidditch.

Magical Creatures

The wizarding world is full of extraordinary creatures. Some of these creatures are friendly while others are dangerous.

Dobby
Dobby is a house-elf.

Troll
During Harry's first year, he and Ron defeat a mountain troll in the girls' bathroom.

Boggart
Neville's Boggart takes the form of Professor Snape.

Acromantula

Norwegian Ridgeback
In Harry's first year, Hagrid takes care of a baby dragon called Norbert.

Thestral
Thestrals pull the
carriages to Hogwarts.

Hippogriff
In Harry's third year, he
and Hermione save a
Hippogriff, called Buckbeak,
from execution.

Phoenix
Dumbledore has a
phoenix called Fawkes.

Fluffy
In Harry's first year, Fluffy
guards the Forbidden
Corridor in Hogwarts.

Werewolf
Professor Lupin
is a werewolf.

Acromantula
Aragog is an Acromantula
—a very large spider.

Basilisk
During Harry's second
year, he battles a Basilisk
in the Chamber of Secrets.

Adventures

Harry and his friends have many adventures. They must use what they have learned in their studies to escape danger.

Lupin's Advice

During Harry's third year, Professor Lupin recommends that Harry eats chocolate after surviving an encounter with a Dementor.

Dementor

Harry first encounters Dementors on the Hogwarts Express during his third year.

Spiders

During their second year, Harry and Ron are surrounded by spiders in the Forbidden Forest.

Fawkes Rescue

Fawkes carries Harry, Ron, Ginny, and Professor Lockhart to safety out of the Basilisk Chamber.

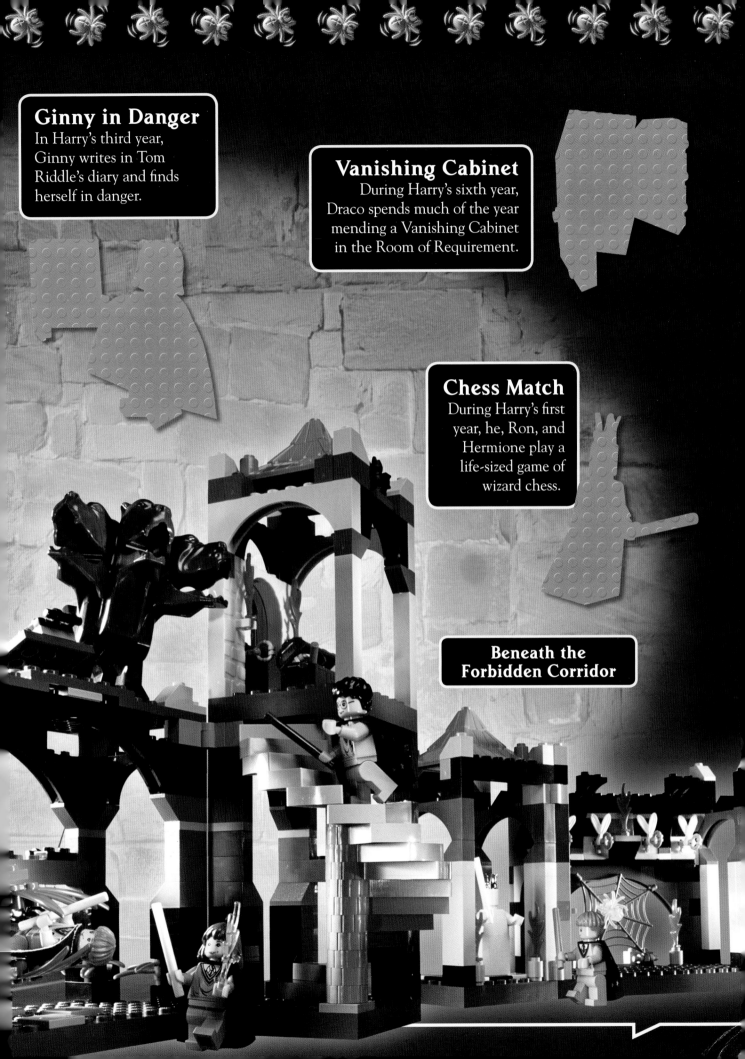

Ginny in Danger
In Harry's third year, Ginny writes in Tom Riddle's diary and finds herself in danger.

Vanishing Cabinet
During Harry's sixth year, Draco spends much of the year mending a Vanishing Cabinet in the Room of Requirement.

Chess Match
During Harry's first year, he, Ron, and Hermione play a life-sized game of wizard chess.

Beneath the Forbidden Corridor

Triwizard Tournament

During Harry's fourth year, the Triwizard Tournament takes place at Hogwarts. Three schools compete to win: Hogwarts, Durmstrang, and Beauxbatons.

Krum in the Second Task
Viktor Krum Transfigures himself into a shark for the second task.

Golden Egg
Harry flies on his broom to retrieve a golden egg.

Hungarian Horntail
The first task of the Triwizard Tournament involves a Hungarian Horntail dragon.

©2011 LEGO

Igor Karkaroff
Igor Karkaroff is the Headmaster of Durmstrang.

Viktor Krum
Viktor Krum is the Durmstrang champion in the Triwizard Tournament.

Durmstrang Ship
The Durmstrang students arrive at Hogwarts on a ship.

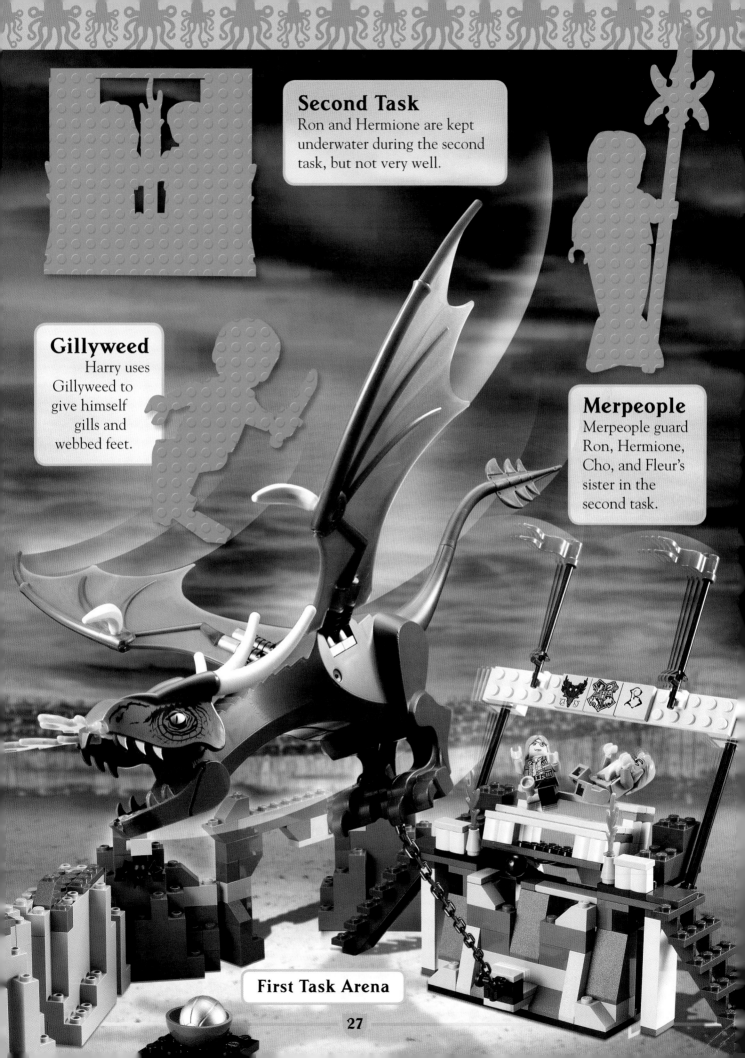

Second Task
Ron and Hermione are kept underwater during the second task, but not very well.

Gillyweed
Harry uses Gillyweed to give himself gills and webbed feet.

Merpeople
Merpeople guard Ron, Hermione, Cho, and Fleur's sister in the second task.

First Task Arena

Dark Arts

Lord Voldemort practices the Dark Arts. He uses the Dark Mark to summon his Death Eaters.

Death Eater
Lord Voldemort's followers wear masks and robes.

He Who Must Not Be Named
Many wizards fear Lord Voldemort and will not utter his name.

BORGIN AND BURKES

Werewolf Fenrir Greyback
Fenrir Greyback appears wolf-like, even when the moon is not full.

Borgin and Burkes

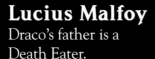

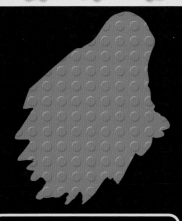

Lucius Malfoy
Draco's father is a Death Eater.

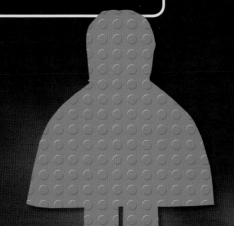

Dementor's Kiss
Dementors make people feel sadness and despair.

Death Eater Draco Malfoy
In Harry's sixth year, Draco Malfoy becomes a Death Eater.

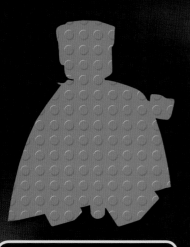

Severus Snape
Severus Snape performs the Unbreakable Vow with Narcissa Malfoy.

Vincent Crabbe
Crabbe is one of Draco Malfoy's cronies.

Gregory Goyle
Goyle is another of Draco's Slytherin cronies.

Bellatrix Lestrange
Bellatrix is a loyal Death Eater.

Peter "Wormtail" Pettigrew
Peter Pettigrew is also known as Wormtail.

Fighting Against Evil

Harry and his friends form Dumbledore's Army in Harry's fifth year. They meet in the Room of Requirement to practice defensive spells.

Albus Dumbledore
Students at Hogwarts name Dumbledore's Army after their Headmaster.

Hermione
Hermione practices spells with Dumbledore's Army.

Fred and George
Fred and George Weasley are proud members of Dumbledore's Army.

Harry
Harry teaches defensive magic to Dumbledore's Army.

Luna
During Dumbledore's Army meetings, Luna learns to cast the Patronus Charm.

Ginny
Ginny Weasley joins her brothers and friends as part of Dumbledore's Army.

Ron
Ron is proud to
fight as part of
Dumbledore's Army.

Neville
Neville finds the Room
of Requirement where
Dumbledore's Army meets.

Hogwarts
Castle

Battle at The Burrow

Bellatrix and Fenrir atttack The Burrow. The Weasleys and Harry battle bravely to save the Weasleys' home.

Bellatrix Lestrange at The Burrow

Bellatrix Lestrange taunts Harry as she and Fenrir Greyback attack The Burrow.

Death Eater Fenrir Greyback

Fenrir Greyback attacks The Burrow with Bellatrix Lestrange.

Mrs. Weasley

Mrs. Weasley defends her family and home from Death Eaters.

Mr. Weasley

Mr. Weasley joins Harry and Ginny in a battle against Bellatrix and Fenrir at The Burrow.

Brave Ginny

Ginny follows Harry through the reeds as fire surrounds The Burrow.

Harry Reacts

Harry Potter races after Bellatrix when she and fellow Death Eaters attack The Burrow.

Dobby

Harry Potter

Mrs. Weasley

Phoenix

Floo Network

Tom Riddle

Knight Bus

Molly Weasley

Neville

Werewolf Fenrir Greyback

Peter "Wormtail" Pettigrew

Parseltongue

Lucius Malfoy

Brave
Ginny

Basilisk

Sorcerer's
Stone

Dementor's Kiss

Norwegian
Ridgeback

Albus Dumbledore

Death Eater
Draco Malfoy

Fluffy

Werewolf

Severus Snape

Tom Riddle's Diary

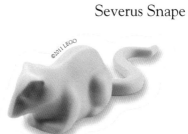

Scabbers

Wizard
Treasure

Ginny Weasley

Death Eater Fenrir Greyback

Bellatrix Lestrange

Fred and George

Mr. Weasley

Bellatrix Lestrange at The Burrow

Harry

Ginny

WIZARD HATS

Harry in Year Four

The Shrieking Shack

Diagon Alley

Fred Weasley

Harry's Wand

Lord Voldemort

George Weasley

Goblin

Hippogriff

Peter Pettigrew

He Who Must Not Be Named

Boggart

4 Privet Drive

Ginger-Haired Ron Weasley

Harry Reacts

Hedwig

Mr. Ollivander

Hermione

Death
Eater

Thestral

Professor Quirrell

Gregory
Goyle

Vincent Crabbe

Arthur
Weasley

CHARACTER WILL BE TESTED

Harry Potter
AND THE PRISONER OF AZKABAN

Honeydukes

Wizard Pets

Ron

Weasleys' Flying Car

Acromantula

Troll

Student Harry

Uncle Vernon

Luna

Stan Shunpike

Riddle's Tomb

YOU WILL LOSE EVERYTHING

Harry Potter
ORDER OF THE PHOENIX

©2011 LEGO

Slytherin Seeker

Top of the Class

Ron Weasley

Professor Snape

Suits of Armor

Dementor

Krum in the Second Task

Sword of Gryffindor

Quidditch Helmet

Chocolate

Merpeople

Crystal Ball

Professor Lupin

Hermione Granger

Professor Flitwick

Ron at Hogwarts

Vanishing
Cabinet

Spiders

Cauldron

Food Trolley

Goalposts

Oliver
Wood

Ready for
School

Time-Turner

Marcus Flint

Draco Malfoy

Marauder's Map

Second Task

Mandrake

Luggage

Lupin's Advice

The Monster
Book of Monsters

Madam Hooch

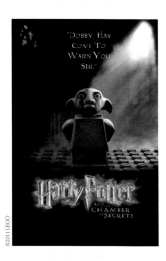

Rubeus Hagrid

Gillyweed

Quidditch Book

Luna Lovegood

Potions

Remembrall

Boat to Hogwarts

Professor Trelawney

Professor Dumbledore

Professor Umbridge

Argus Filch

Invisibility Cloak

Trunks

Golden
Egg

Mirror
of Erised

Quidditch
Cup

Golden
Snitch

HOGSMEADE™

Chess
Match

Transfiguration

Durmstrang Ship

LEGO Harry Potter

Dumbledore's Chocolate Frog Card

Hogwarts
Acceptance Letter

Neville Longbottom

Fawkes
Rescue

Hungarian Horntail

Ginny in Danger

Harry at Hogwarts

Best Friend
Ron Weasley

Firebolt

Quidditch Balls

Seeker

Winged Key

Igor Karkaroff

Viktor Krum

Professor McGonagall

Studying

Harry Potter
GOBLET FIRE
DARK AND DIFFICULT TIMES LIE AHEAD

Professor Lockhart

Four Houses

The Sorting Hat

EXTRA STICKERS

EXTRA STICKERS

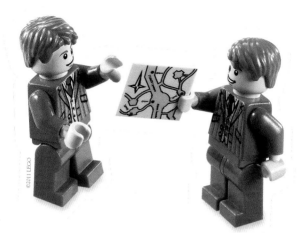

CHARACTER WILL BE TESTED

Harry Potter
AND THE PRISONER OF AZKABAN

EXTRA STICKERS

©2011 LEGO

©2011 LEGO

©2011 LEGO

©2011 LEGO

©2011 LEGO

©2011 LEGO

©2011 LEGO

©2011 LEGO

©2011 LEGO

©2011 LEGO

©2011 LEGO

©2011 LEGO

"DOBBY HAS COME TO WARN YOU SIR."

Harry Potter
AND THE
CHAMBER OF SECRETS

EXTRA STICKERS

EXTRA STICKERS